**DO NOT REMOVE
CARDS FROM POCKET**

The Turnip

A Puffin Easy-to-Read Classic

retold by Harriet Ziefert
illustrated by Laura Rader

PUFFIN BOOKS

PUFFIN BOOKS

Published by the Penguin Group

Penguin Books USA Inc., 375 Hudson Street, New York, New York 10014, U.S.A.

Penguin Books Ltd, 27 Wrights Lane, London W8 5TZ, England

Penguin Books Australia Ltd, Ringwood, Victoria, Australia

Penguin Books Canada Ltd, 10 Alcorn Avenue, Toronto, Ontario, Canada M4V 3B2

Penguin Books (N.Z.) Ltd, 182–190 Wairau Road, Auckland 10, New Zealand

Penguin Books Ltd, Registered Offices: Harmondsworth, Middlesex, England

First published in the United States of America by Viking,
a division of Penguin Books USA Inc., 1996

Published simultaneously in Puffin Books

1 3 5 7 9 10 8 6 4 2

Text copyright © Harriet Ziefert, 1996
Illustrations copyright © Laura Rader, 1996
All rights reserved

THE LIBRARY OF CONGRESS HAS CATALOGED THE VIKING EDITION AS FOLLOWS:

Ziefert, Harriet.
The turnip / retold by Harriet Ziefert; illustrated by Laura Rader.
p. cm.—(Viking easy-to-read)
"A Viking easy-to-read classic."
Summary: One of the old man's turnips grows to such an enormous size that
he needs the help of his wife, a little girl, a dog, a cat, and a mouse to pull it up.
ISBN 0-670-86053-0
[1. Folklore—Russia.] I. Rader, Laura, ill. II. Title. III. Series.
PZ8.1.Z55Tu 1996 398.2'0947'02—dc20 [E] 95-39340 CIP AC

Puffin Books ISBN 0-14-038082-5

Printed in the United States of America

Puffin® and Easy-to-Read® are registered trademarks of Penguin Books USA Inc.

Reading Level 1.5

The Turnip

An old man planted
a little turnip.

"Grow, grow, little turnip.
Grow sweet," he said.
"Grow, grow, little turnip.
Grow big."

The little turnip grew
sweet and big.

One day the old man
went to pull the turnip up.

He pulled and pulled.
But he could not pull it up.

He called the old woman.

The old woman pulled the old man.
The old man pulled the turnip.

They pulled and pulled.
But they could not pull it up.

Yoo

The old woman called
the little girl.

hoo!

The little girl pulled the old woman.
The old woman pulled the old man.
The old man pulled the turnip.

They pulled and pulled.
But they could not pull it up.

The little girl called
the big dog.

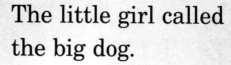

The big dog pulled the girl.
The girl pulled the old woman.
The old woman pulled the old man.
The old man pulled the turnip.

They pulled and pulled.
But they could not pull it up.

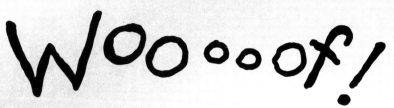

The dog called the cat.

The cat pulled the dog.
The dog pulled the girl.
The girl pulled the old woman.
The old woman pulled the old man.
The old man pulled the turnip.

They pulled and pulled.
But they could not pull it up.

The cat called the tiny mouse.

The mouse pulled the cat.
The cat pulled the dog.
The dog pulled the girl.

The girl pulled the old woman.
The old woman pulled the old man.
The old man pulled the turnip.

They pulled and pulled and pulled.

And up came the turnip!